Starlight Grey

To Molly and Hanna — L. F.
For Delfina and Felipe, with love from Auntie Vale — V. D.

Barefoot Books
294 Banbury Road
Oxford, OX2 7ED

Graphic design by Love Has No Logic Design Group, Chicago, USA
Colour separation by B & P International, Hong Kong
Printed in China on 100% acid-free paper
This book was typeset in Albemarle, Bembo Infant and Captain Kidd
The illustrations were prepared in gouache paints and finished digitally

The editors would like to thank Year 2 at St Mary and
All Saints School for all their careful reading.

Source:
Riordan, James. 'Chestnut Grey.'
Tales from Central Russia.
London: Viking, 1976.

ISBN 978-1-84686-777-4

British Cataloguing-in-Publication Data:
a catalogue record for this book is available
from the British Library

1 3 5 7 9 8 6 4 2

Starlight
Grey

A Story from Russia

Retold by Liz Flanagan
Illustrated by Valeria Docampo

Barefoot Books
step inside a story

CONTENTS

CHAPTER 1
Ivan the Dreamer

Long ago in Russia, there was an old farmer who had three sons. The two oldest boys were tall, handsome and hardworking. The youngest boy was not.

His name was Ivan. He was short
and scruffy. He was not handsome or
hardworking. He spent all of his time
sitting by the fire and dreaming.

One day, the old man said to his sons, 'When I die, you must each take turns sitting by my grave for one night. Promise me that you will do this.'

'We promise,' said the old man's three sons.

A few months later, the old man died.

His three sons were very sad. They buried

him and wept at his grave.

That night, the oldest son was too
scared to keep his promise. He went to Ivan
and said, 'I don't want to sit by our father's
grave. You go instead.'

'I will,' Ivan agreed.

It was dark when Ivan went out, but the
moon and the stars were bright. Ivan sat
down at his father's grave and waited.

At midnight, the ghost of Ivan's father appeared. Ivan's legs shook and he wanted to run away. Then he said to himself, 'Why should I be afraid of my own father?'

The ghost asked, 'Who is there? Is it my oldest son?'

'No, Father. It's Ivan,' he replied, and he stayed where he was.

The ghost asked,

> 'How is life in Russia?
> Do dogs bark on the hill?
> Do wolves howl in the forest?
> And do my sons weep still?'

Ivan said, 'All is well, Father. Rest in peace.'

Then the ghost disappeared and Ivan went home.

CHAPTER 2

The Magic Bridle

The next evening, it was the second
brother's turn to sit by the grave. He also
was too frightened to go. So he went to
Ivan and said, 'I don't want to sit by our
father's grave. You go instead.'

'I will,' Ivan agreed again.

It was dark when Ivan went out, but the moon and the stars were bright. Ivan sat down at his father's grave and waited.

Just as before, the ghost of Ivan's father appeared at midnight. And just as before, Ivan spoke to his father's ghost. Then he returned home safely.

On the third night, Ivan went back to
the grave for the last time. At the stroke of
midnight, the ghost appeared again. It came
very close to Ivan and gave him a gift.

The ghost said, 'You were not afraid,

Ivan. You were the only one to keep your

promise. Take this magic bridle. If ever you

need help, go out onto the plain. Call these

words: "Starlight Grey! Hear and obey!"

'A horse will appear. Put the bridle on
the horse's head and then climb into one of
its ears and out of the other. Then get on
the horse and ride wherever you must go.'

Ivan took the bridle and thanked his father. They said goodbye to each other for the last time. Then the ghost disappeared forever. Ivan went home and hid the bridle in his room.

The two oldest brothers forgot all about
their father. They worked hard and became
rich. Ivan stayed at home. He spent all of
his time sitting by the fire and dreaming.

CHAPTER 3
The King's Announcement

One day, the king sent a message to all the young men in the land. He asked them to come to his palace.

The king had a daughter. She was a
very beautiful princess. She had promised
to marry the man who could leap up to
her window and kiss her. That might sound
easy, but it was not. The princess's window
was at the top of a very high tower. The
tower was made of twelve rows of oak logs.

'Let's go to the king's palace,' Ivan's
brothers said. They put on their best clothes.
They led out their fastest horses. They fed
the horses on oats to make them run fast
and jump high.

'Please take me with you,' Ivan begged
his brothers.

'You can't come!' they laughed at him
unkindly. 'Look at you! You are filthy and
you have no horse.'

After his brothers had left, Ivan took out the magic bridle from its hiding place. He went out to the plain and called, 'Starlight Grey! Hear and obey!'

Just as his father had promised, a horse appeared.

And what a horse it was! Its coat
sparkled like starlight. It snorted hot
flames from its nose. Smoke spilled from
its ears. The ground shook as it galloped
towards Ivan.

The horse stopped in front of Ivan and
said, 'I'm Starlight Grey. I hear and obey.
What is your wish?'

Ivan remembered his father's words.

He put the magic bridle on the horse and climbed into one of its ears. Then he climbed out of the other ear.

He had completely changed!

Now Ivan was dressed in fine clothes of red and gold. Now he was a handsome knight!

Quickly, Ivan sprang up onto the horse's back. 'To the palace!' he cried.

CHAPTER 4

The Princess
in the Tower

As fast as lightning, Starlight Grey

galloped past mountains, forests and lakes.

Soon Starlight Grey and Ivan arrived at the

king's palace.

Ivan saw crowds of people in front of
the princess's tower. It was very high and the
princess was very beautiful.

The king came out. He told the crowds,
'If any man can leap up and kiss my
daughter on the lips, she will marry him.
You may each have three chances.'

There was a long line of strong, brave, young men. Ivan saw his brothers near the front. All the young men took turns to try and reach the princess. But no one could do it. The tower made of twelve rows of oak logs was too high.

Then it was Ivan's turn. He gave a great
shout. Starlight Grey leapt up. Higher and
higher and higher he went. But Ivan only
reached the tenth row of logs. Ivan spun his
horse around and tried again.

Starlight Grey leapt higher still.
Up and up and up he went. But Ivan
only reached the eleventh row of logs.

Ivan had one last chance. He let
out a great roar. Starlight Grey
jumped higher than ever. Flames
flickered from his mouth.

Ivan stretched up and kissed the princess on the lips. As he kissed her, the princess touched the top of Ivan's head with her ruby ring. The ring left a red circle on his forehead.

The crowd clapped and cheered.

'Who is the mysterious knight?' people
asked. 'Stop him!'

But Ivan and Starlight Grey had
galloped away.

When they reached the plain,
Ivan climbed back through his horse's
ears. He was the same old, ordinary
Ivan again. He took off Starlight
Grey's bridle and set him free. Ivan
covered his forehead with an old rag
to hide the red circle.

CHAPTER 5

The King's Feast

Ivan's brothers returned home.

They were excited to share their news.

'Oh Ivan, what a princess! She is more

beautiful than the stars,' they said.

'There was one brave knight who
reached up high enough to kiss the princess,'
they went on. 'You should have seen his
horse! He deserves to marry her. But he
vanished like smoke in the wind.'

Ivan said, 'Perhaps it was me who kissed the princess.'

That made his brothers furious. 'You're nothing but a fool and a dreamer,' they said.

Ivan only smiled and curled up by the fire to sleep.

The next day, the king invited every single person in the land to a great feast. Rich and poor, young and old — everybody went to the palace.

Ivan's brothers got ready to leave. 'Take me with you,' Ivan begged them.

'You? You can't come. People would only laugh at you,' they said. And they pushed him back to his place by the fire.

Ivan followed them on foot, carrying the magic bridle. He hid the bridle in the corner of the king's great hall.

The princess went round to each guest and
said, 'Would you like a drink from my cup?'

As they drank from her golden goblet,
she looked carefully at each person's forehead.
She was searching for the red circle from her
ruby ring.

Finally, there was only one person
left. The princess looked at Ivan with his
scruffy clothes and his dirty face. She looked
at his head tied with an old rag.

'Why is your head tied with a rag?' she
asked him kindly.

Ivan replied, 'I fell from my horse and
hurt myself.'

'Let me see,' the princess said. She gently
untied the rag. The circle on Ivan's forehead
glowed bright red. The light filled the hall
and everyone turned to stare.

The king stepped between
Ivan and the princess. 'This must
be a mistake,' he said. 'He can't be
your husband. Just look at him!'

Ivan stood up. 'Let me go and wash,'
he said. The king happily let Ivan leave.

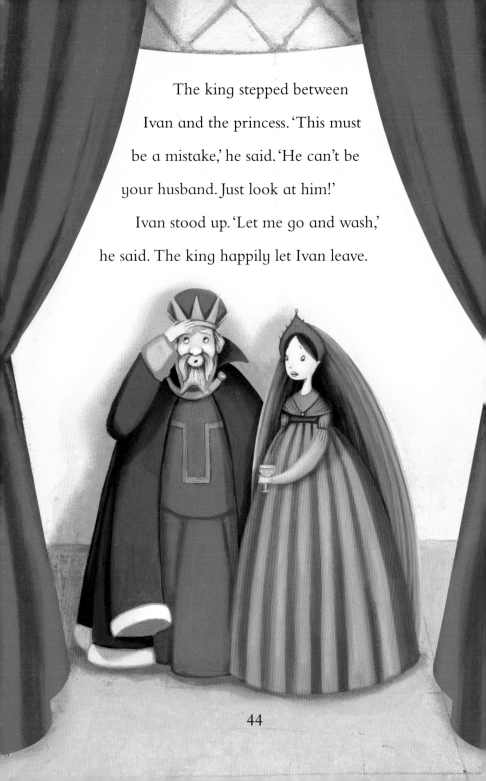

Ivan went outside and called, 'Starlight
Grey! Hear and obey!' The ground shook.
Starlight Grey galloped up. He stood there,
snorting fire and pouring smoke.

Ivan climbed into one ear and out of
the other. He was a fine knight again.

Ivan walked back into
the hall. He was changed, but
the red circle still glowed on his
forehead. All the guests gasped.

Ivan's own brothers
were astonished. 'Ivan!
You were the mysterious
knight who kissed the princess!'
And they fell on their knees. 'We're
sorry!' they said.

Ivan and the princess were married.
They loved each other very much and were
happy for the rest of their lives. Together
they rode Starlight Grey far and wide and
saw all the wonders of the world.